Faded Men: Chaison and Maison

By Candi Usher

Table of Contents

Table of Contents _____ *2*

Wash _____ *3*

Blowdry _____ *10*

Comb _____ *22*

Oil _____ *33*

Trim the Ends _____ *40*

Discuss a Style _____ *51*

Braided Up _____ *63*

Beard Gang _____ *73*

Fresh _____ *84*

Wash

Sha'nae stood there, rubbing her very pregnant stomach. She knew the babies she carried were important. The Covenant made that apparent the moment they found out she was pregnant. The thing was, she still couldn't remember how she ended up pregnant. Her husband, Darius, said it happened one night when she had taken her sleep medicine. She woke up in the hospital later that night. Sha'nae didn't remember. She felt like something had been stolen from her; she just didn't know what it was.

The Covenant was a cult that Darius and Sha'nae had joined. Sha'nae was following Darius. They had been married for 5 years. They were struggling with infertility. As much as they wanted a baby, it just wasn't happening naturally. Darius had been introduced to the Covenant as a group that wanted to help couples with infertility. They had a hospital and all the needed doctors. The Covenant promised couples would have a baby within one year based on the treatments they offered.

Darius had attended the meetings. Sha'nae didn't feel comfortable going. Something about the group just felt off. She couldn't put her finger on what. Sha'nae did her research about the group, but she didn't find much. There were brochures about the Covenant. They looked to be normal. Sha'nae felt uncomfortable. Darius asked how the Covenant could help them, so Sha'nae stopped arguing. She wanted to be a mother, so she hid her feelings and agreed with her husband.

    Three months after going to the Covenant treatment center, Sha'nae discovered she was pregnant. She and Darius were so excited. Then Darius began to pull away from Sha'nae. It was as if she had become repulsive to him. Sha'nae couldn't understand what was happening. Something was weird. Darius wouldn't explain anything. She felt he knew something that he couldn't or wouldn't tell her. Sha'nae wanted to leave the Covenant. She just didn't know how she would do it. She hoped for a plan to come soon.

    The Covenant was off the grid. It was in a forest that apparently the city or county didn't care about. Not many people went in and out. There were selected people to get food, pay bills, and do anything else that required leaving. All of Sha'nae's doctor's appointments were held in the small hospital room on the campus. The doctor never seemed to be the same every visit. Sha'nae also found that odd, but it was another thing she couldn't find the answer to.

    The plan came to Sha'nae sooner than she expected. She was in her and Darius's room, lying in bed. One moment, she was rubbing her stomach; the next, sharp pain went through her back and abdomen. Sha'nae was bent over in pain. Her water broke, but there was blood in it. She began to panic.

"Darius!! Something's wrong!!" Sha'nae screamed. Darius didn't run into the room at her scream. Another dweller did. Sha'nae didn't want anyone else near her. She tried to call Darius, but he wasn't answering Sha'nae's call. She eventually allowed the other dweller to help her to the small hospital.

"Help!! She needs help!!" The dweller yelled when they arrived.

"My babies!!" Sha'nae was starting to panic even more.

"It looks like one of the babies is breech and has pulled at the placenta. We need to get you to a bigger hospital!" The doctor said with determination. He was going to make sure these babies were safely born. The leader commanded him to make sure. He cared nothing about the mother. These babies were unique, and the Leader wanted them.

"Let's get her to a bigger hospital. She's going to need a C-section." The nurse called out. Sha'nae realized she was about to leave, and Darius was nowhere to be found. As Sha'nae was wheeled to the waiting ambulance, she saw Darius hugging another woman. Sha'nae was broken but didn't have time to focus as another pain ripped through her, robbing her of her voice and breath.

"Please hurry!" She thought to herself, hoping that her babies would be ok. She didn't know what they were considering the limitations of the clinic on campus.

The leader was notified that Sha'nae was in labor but needed to go to the city hospital because of complications. He smiled to himself. Things were starting to heat up. Those babies would be the lifeline he needed later. No one knew his plans because not everyone could be trusted. He knew some would try to destroy his plan if they found out. The future was about to be born.

Sha'nae arrived at the hospital 15 minutes later. The pain had become intense. She was rushed to the room for immediate surgery. The last thing Sha'nae remembered was being told to breathe deeply after a mask was placed over her face. She woke up to the cries of her babies. "Bring me my babies. I want to see them." Sha'nae requested. The nurse looked slightly leery but took the babies to their mother at the doctor's instructions. Sha'nae held her babies close. She checked to see if they were boys or girls. She noticed she had identical twin boys. As Sha'nae shushed them, one opened their eyes to look straight into hers.

"Oh My GOD!!! Why? Why are your eyes like this? These can't be my babies. They can't be!!" Sha'nae was confused. She knew that she and Darius had brown eyes. He had brown eyes and black hair. They both had brown skin. The babies were both medium-skinned and had an eye color that Sha'nae had only seen once.

"Was I carrying these babies for someone else? What did those people do to me?" Sha'nae couldn't get the thoughts out of her head. She thought of a way to leave the hospital and take her sons elsewhere. She couldn't take them back to the Covenant. Something was wrong with that place, and she didn't want her sons to grow up in that environment. Sha'nae grabbed the phone to make a call.

"Hello," said a voice that Sha'nae had missed with her whole heart.

"Hey, sis. I need your help. How soon can you get to me? I'm in a hospital in Covenant. I'll send you the address." Sha'nae tried to keep herself calm.

"Sure!! Where are we going?" The voice answered.

"I don't know yet. I just need to get out of here first." Sha'nae explained.

"By the way, why are you in the hospital?" The voice asked, sounding surprised.

"I just had identical twins. The thing is, they don't look much like me and nothing like their father. I think the place that helped us get pregnant is on something shady; I just don't know yet. I need to leave. I don't think me nor my babies are safe here." Sha'nae said, trying not to panic again. Panicking would do nothing for her or the babies. Her mind needed to be clear and focused.

"I'm on my way. Do you need car seats?" The other person asked.

"Yeah. And get some clothes for the babies. Preferably something that doesn't show that they're boys. Hey, I gotta go. The nurse is coming in, and I don't trust her. Hurry up and get here." Sha'nae was trying to hide what she was doing.

The other voice answered, "Hang on, twin." I'm on my way!!"

Blowdry

    Sha'nae's identical twin sister, Sha'ree, arrived in record time. She ran into the hospital, jumped into the elevator, and walked quickly to the room number Sha'nae had given her. As soon as Sha'nae saw her, she started bawling.
"I missed you too, Twin," Sha'ree said, comforting her sister.
"I'm so sorry. I'm sorry that I left. I'm sorry that I didn't call. I'm so, so sorry!!" Sha'nae was almost wailing.
"Girl, if you don't put the shut to the up before you wake up my nephews," Sha'ree shushed her.
"My bad. I'm just so happy to see you!! Did you say anything to mom or dad?" Sha'nae asked.
Sha'ree shook her head. "They can find out when we get back to Chiva. I have a house you can stay in that would be safe for you and the babies. Girl, what happened? Why are you so freaked out?"
Sha'nae pointed to the babies. "Go look at their eyes."
Sha'ree walked over slowly, scared of what she might find. At that moment, both twins stopped fussing and looked right into their aunt's eyes.
"Oh, heck no!!! Why the baby's eyes look like that? Girl, who is your baby daddy? I thought you

and Darius were married. Something here ain't right." Sha'ree was about ready to run out of the room. She wanted no part of a conspiracy.
Sha'nae shook her head. "This is what I'm scared of. I think the Covenant did something to me. There was a night when I fell asleep and then woke up in this very hospital. Darius said he was scared because I was sleeping too deeply from the sleep medicine. I don't sleep to the point where I can't wake up from the medicine. I think I was drugged. On top of that, on the way here, I saw Darius with another woman. I believe that our marriage is over. "
"After all of this, I would say so. He didn't even try to find you?' Sha'ree was getting heated over how her twin was being treated. Things didn't sit right with her either.
Sha'nae shook her head. "No, and I don't want Darius to. I want a clean divorce. Can you help me with that?" Sha'nae and Sha'ree had gone to college to study law. Sha'nae didn't finish because she was stuck on Darius halfway through college. Sha'ree, on the other hand, dated, but she wasn't about to let anyone stand in the way of getting her degree and passing the bar.
"You know I got you sis. What are my nephews' names?" Sha'ree asked.

"Chaison in the quieter one. That hollering one is Maison. They are opposites. I'm sure Maison was probably the one tearing up my ribs and back. The child is vicious already." Sha'nae looked over at her sons. Despite what was going on, she was in love with her babies. She would protect them at any cost. Sha'nae knew Sha'ree would too. Their parents were a toss-up. But the twins figured they would come around once their grandsons were in their arms.

    The nurse came in with a pot of geraniums. She placed them on the table next to the hospital bed. The nurse then pulled out a tablet, checking and entering Sha'nae's vitals. She then walked over to the babies, checked them, entered the information, and left. She said nothing to anyone in the room. Sha'ree didn't feel comfortable with the nurse. She turned to say something to her twin when she saw tears running down Sha'nae's face. "What's wrong?" Sha'ree was almost screaming. "That was her. That was the woman Darius was hugging when I was placed in the ambulance. This was on purpose!! I have to get out of here!!" Sha'nae was ready to leave. She had to get out of that hospital and that town. She needed to protect her sons.

"Ummm .... geraniums aren't normal to be given as a present, are they?" Sha'ree was confused. She hurried and Googled what geraniums meant. "Geraniums mean stupidity, folly. Why would Darius send you some flowers like that? Where is that idiot??!!" Sha'ree was livid!! She already didn't like Darius marrying her sister and taking her away. Now he was cheating on Sha'nae and had his little girlfriend checking on her sister? Sha'ree was not having it. She would break him in two before he would destroy her twin. Sha'ree wanted to get her sister and her nephews out of that hospital and that town.

"Sha'nae, what will it take to get you checked out? Like, what do you need to be signed out of here? I don't think you're safe anymore. Something isn't normal. I don't feel right." Sha'ree wanted to move. She felt the nurse was coming to see who was in the room, not necessarily checking on Sha'nae and the babies.

"I have to have a doctor sign me out. I don't know if one will. The doctors and nurses are working for the Covenant. These babies belong to their leader. They aren't going to let me leave that easily." Sha'nae felt lost. She wanted to protect her babies. She returned to the plan she had started before giving birth to the babies. Sha'nae knew what she had to do.

"Sha'ree, I need you to take the twins and leave. Take them as far away from here as possible. Protect them. Don't let the Covenant get them."
Sha'ree shook her head. "I can't do that. They need you!! I can't do this without you!!" She was on the verge of tears. She couldn't let her twin get hurt. Sha'nae had just come back into her life. The phone call earlier that day was the first time they had talked in almost a year. Sha'ree knew that Sha'nae wasn't just asking her because they were twins but because she knew Sha'ree would protect the twin with her life.
"Are the car seats in the car?" Sha'nae asked.
"Yes. They are locked in and ready. Why?" Sha'ree was nervous yet ready.
"Pull your car to the front. I'm going to dress the babies. After you pull the car to the front, meet me in the bathroom. That way, the cameras can't see. I will take Chaison and Maison in like I'm going to bathe them. Come in, and I will give them to you. Place them in your jacket and walk out. The babies are small enough not to be seen. Take them away. Please Sha'ree. Take care of my babies!!" Sha'nae begged.

Sha'ree couldn't process what her sister was saying to her. She wanted her to do what? Why was she asking her to take the babies away? Where was Sha'ree going to take them? She shook her head vehemently, trying not to acknowledge what her sister asked her.
"Are you crazy? Sha'nae, I can't do this by myself. You have to come with me. Chaison and Maison need you!!" Sha'ree was starting to feel a bit hysterical. She wanted to help her sisters and her nephews.
"Sha'ree, you have to do this. Their protection is the most important thing to me. Please!!" Sha'nae was on the verge of tears. She couldn't become too hysterical, or it would cause the babies more distress. Sha'nae understood that Sha'ree was scared. She was, too. But they had to get their heads together. Time was running out. Sha'nae didn't know if the nurse was reporting to someone.
"Sha'ree, go do what I said. Make sure the car seats are locked in well. I already have their bath ready. I'm going to get the twins ready."

Sha'ree's brain stopped working at that moment. She went into survival mode. She almost ran down the hall, glancing around her occasionally to ensure she didn't look suspicious. Sha'ree turned the corner to the left. She had to walk past the maternity ward desk to the hospital's front doors. As she turned, Sha'ree saw the nurse who had just checked on Sha'nae. She noticed the nurse was on the phone. Sha'nae moved closer to hear what she was saying.

"Yes, Elder. I understand. Ms. Mope has had the babies. I'm waiting for her to rest and return the babies to the campus. There was another woman in there, though. She looked just like Ms. Mope. I don't feel comfortable with that, Sir." The nurse gave whoever was on the other end of the line a rundown of what was happening. Sha'nae realized that she would have to create a distraction and speed things up. Her sister and her nephews were not safe.

"Oh, and I did get some of the medicine you asked me to get. Ms. Mope will be incapacitated for a while. When do you want her brought to you? This first trial was successful. She carried the babies well. Ms. Mope seems to be the perfect candidate for your bloodline. No one else has managed to carry that long. The twins look exactly like you, also. Yes, Sir. I understand, Elder. I will get things in motion as soon as I finish updating the chart and talking to the doctor. Be well, Elder." The nurse hung up the phone and then returned to the computer before her. Sha'ree crept past the desk, then sped up to go out the doors.

Sha'ree was glad she parked her SUV near the front doors. She hurried to the truck, ensured the car seats were correctly locked, and crunk up the SUV. Sha'ree remembered to look for cameras. She needed to be able to leave as soon as Sha'nae handed her Chaison and Maison. Sha'ree carefully pulled her SUV past the front doors. The few cameras she did see made her nervous. If this went well, Sha'ree could get Sha'nae and the babies safely out of there. As Sha'ree walked back inside and got ready to sneak past the desk again, she saw the nurse get up and head down the hall. Sha'ree walked behind her quietly, not to arouse suspicion, but still kept an eye on whether she was headed toward Sha'nae's room, precisely where the nurse went.

The nurse knocked on the door. "Ms. Mope. Can I come in?" There was no sound heard from the other side. Sha'ree stood just across the hall in case Sha'nae needed her. The nurse pushed open the door. Sha'ree hurried to Sha'nae's room. She heard a ping and then a thunk. Sha'nae saw the nurse lying on the floor. She hurried up and shut the door before someone came to investigate. Fortunately, the maternity floor wasn't very busy, so there weren't too many people walking back and forth.

"You knocked the mess out of her!!" Sha'ree whispered loudly while giggling.

"Really, Sha'ree? That's what you're worried about right now?" Sha'nae knew her twin could be a little ditzy when being nervous. But she needed her to focus. They had to hurry before the nurse woke or someone came looking for her. Sha'nae gave Sha'ree a stern look, which calmed her down and got her moving.

"Where do you want me to put this big heifa at? She weighs about three freaking tons." Sha'ree was huffing and puffing hard. The twins looked into each other's faces and burst out laughing. They hadn't laughed like that in so long. Sha'ree missed Sha'nae so much. There were so many things they needed to discuss. Once they got the babies to safety, Sha'ree wanted to fill Sha'nae with some things that had been happening to her. She had already prepped herself to be ready to get chewed out.

"Drag her to the other side of the bed. I have the baby bag ready. There's enough diapers and formula to last for a couple of weeks. I'm sending you my ID, too. You're going to need it to get the boys their formula." Sha'nae sounded really tired.

Sha'ree had a feeling things were not going to go good. At that moment, someone came knocking at the door. "Who is it?" Sha'nae yelled.
"Is Nurse Myers in there?" A deep voice called from the other side of the door.
"No, she isn't. I'm resting and feeding my babies. Can you come back a little later?" Sha'nae called. She and Sha'ree heard footsteps walk away. Both went to peek out the door and ensure the coast was clear. They both sighed in relief that the person was gone.
Sha'nae started to shake a little. "Ok, now that Nurse Myers is out the way, what next?"
Sha'ree walked to the bed where the twins were lying. "Place one twin on each side of your chest. It's cool enough outside that no one will notice your jacket is a little thick. Both of them have been fed and changed, so neither should start fussing. I just changed so I can follow behind you." Sha'ree didn't know that Sha'nae had no plans to follow her. She needed to stop whoever was trying to take her babies. Sha'nae knew she would need to make a sacrifice. There was an advantage to having an identical twin.
"Ok," Sha'nae answered, placing Maison on the front right side of her jacket, then tucked Chaison

on the other side. "Does this look ok? Can you see anything?"

Sha'nae shook her head, emotions starting to take their toll on her. It was becoming a reality that she may never see her babies again. She took a deep breath.

"Hurry up and start walking," Sha'ree demanded as she put the baby bag on Sha'nae's shoulder. She slid her shoes on her feet, checking to make sure Nurse Myers was still out. She was going to have a nasty little knot on her head later. Ms. Thing deserved it after messing with Darius in front of her. She wanted to clock him, too, but that could wait until another date. Sha'ree pushed Sha'nae down the hall. Suddenly, the head doctor came around the corner. Sha'ree hurried to him. "Hey, Doctor Samuel. I have a couple of questions about the babies. Do you think you could help me?" Sha'nae stepped on the doctor's path, then signaled to Sha'ree to keep walking. Sha'ree moved faster before the sudden noise could wake the twins.

Sha'ree got to the SUV, taking Maison out first. He weirded her out just a little. Maison always seemed to judge or be mad at you with his eyes. Chaison, on the other hand, barely moved when he was taken out of the jacket and placed in his car seat. Sha'ree covered both babies with the blankets she had purchased. She hurried to the driver's door and jumped into the SUV. Suddenly, her phone pinged.

"You've got to go!!" The message read. "They're looking for the babies right now. My distraction is only going to work for a few more minutes. Go!! I'll check in with you shortly. I love you, sis. So much!!" The screen went blank. Sha'ree tried to wrap her mind around what had happened. She wanted to go back in and get Sha'nae. But if she did, it would leave the babies exposed, which Sha'ree knew Sha'nae didn't want her to do. Sha'ree cranked up the SUV and drove off, tears running down her face. She hated the Covenant, and she hated even more what was done to her sister and her babies. The further away Sha'ree drove, the more her heart ached.

Comb

Sha'nae sent the text, then closed her phone. "There. She's gone, and the babies are gone. So, what do you want from me, Xavior? I know you're missing my sister. Why are you even here?" Sha'nae knew that Sha'ree would recognize Xavior if she saw him. He was supposed to have died in a plane crash the year before. It was an intentional plan. Xavior's father was associated with the Covenant cult in some form. Sha'nae didn't know the connection and didn't want to know. All she knew was that her twin had been in love with him, and it broke her to see her sister hurt like that.

Xavior shook his head. "You know this had to be done. My dad and Xavion won't stop until they get what they want."

"And what exactly do they want? What does it have to do with Sha'ree? There's something you're not telling me, Xavior." Sha'nae found herself growing angry.

"Don't come at me with that mess, Nae. You know I loved Ree with everything inside me. Now, I'm trying to protect both of you and those babies. My dad is up to no good. I need time to figure out what's going on." Xavior wasn't trying to become agitated. He just wanted to discover why so many things were happening—the creation of Maison and Chaison. What did the cult need them for? Who was running the cult? Why did the cult leader want him dead?

"I need to get out of here!! Are you going to help or what?" Sha'nae was running out of patience. Xavior shook his head. "I can't help you with that. No one but you know I'm still alive. It has to stay that way so I can protect your twins." Sha'nae rolled her eyes. It looked like she would have to return to the Covenant Campus for a while. She wanted to find out what was happening with Darius and Nurse Myers. There were still no pieces matching this puzzle. It was becoming more and more frustrating. Sha'nae was more scared now than ever. She hoped Sha'ree would get far enough away that no one from Covenant could reach her. Patience was going to have to become a virtue. Just then, Xavior took off. Sha'nae looked around to see what was going on. At that very exact moment, a needle was stuck in the side of her throat. As Sha'nae fell, she caught a glimpse of Nurse Myer's face.

"So, you just gone hit me upside the head with that little bedpan, huh? You better be glad Elder wants you for some more babies. Otherwise, you wouldn't be leaving this hospital!!" Nurse Myers stood over Sha'nae. The last thing she heard before passing out was Nurse Myers calling Darius to help her move her.

****

Xavior hurried out of the hospital. That was way too close. He wanted to protect Sha'nae and Sha'ree. Xavior always found it odd that his dad had wanted to move him and his twin to Covenant. It was a little podunk town with a weird smell and even weirder people. They had moved there when Xavior was twelve. He and his identical twin Xavion supposedly lost their mother right after they were born. The thing is, in all the years Xavior had been doing research, there was nothing that indicated that their mother was dead.

Things were happening too strangely. The disappearance of his mother, Sha'nae having the twins, and someone trying to kill him and Sha'ree was too coincidental. Xavior wanted to say something to Sha'nae about the twins, but he felt it was best not to yet. Their eye color signified way more than Sha'nae could wrap her mind around. Oddly, their eyes were the same color as Xavior's father's eyes- and the eyes of both him and his brother. Xavior and his brother each had one purple eye and one golden eye. It was a combination no one had. That's why Xavior believed that some modification was made to create him and his twin, then Sha'nae's twins. He felt Darius was in on it also, just not how much. Xavior and his brother had grown up with Darius. Xavion had liked Sha'ree. Darius made a move on Sha'nae so he could keep Xavion from using her to get close to Sha'ree. Darius' jealousy was nasty. That man could destroy some things when angry.

Xavior and Xavion's father took Darius in after he was abandoned by some people at the Covenant. No one knew who his parents were. There were no clues as to where he came from. Xavior tried to look into things, but it seemed any files were carefully hidden or destroyed. Lives were being manipulated, and Xavior needed to know why. He wanted to contact Sha'ree but knew that would be another dangerous game. She needed to keep believing he was dead. It was the only thing that would keep her off Xion's radar.

***

Sha'nae was taken back to the Covenant campus. She knew that the Elder wanted to see her. She wanted to see what he looked like. It felt like there was more to the issue than what was on the surface. She had received a text from Sha'nae saying that Nurse Myers mentioned trying to impregnate some other women before, but the pregnancies all failed. What would be the reason for doing all of that? Primarily through a facility that was supposed to be helping people with fertility between their spouse or significant other, not using them as guinea pigs.

 Sha'nae's wheelchair was pushed into an office building at the back of the campus. She had never seen this building before. It looks old, though. Nurse Myers was being intentionally rough. Still big mad about being hit upside the head. Sha'nae would have hit her again if she had the strength. She didn't know what was in that syringe, but it overrode everything she was trying to tell her body to do. Sha'nae's arms and legs wouldn't move. She could breathe but couldn't move her lips. Her body felt light and heavy at the same time.

"You deserve every bit of this." Nurse Myers fumed. "I hope Elder punishes you in the worst way possible. Gone hit me, and think you get away with it." Myers was still on a roll. Sha'nae just wished she would put the shut to the up. Her voice was mad annoying.

"Shut upp," Sha'nae tried to move her lips.

"Who you think you talking to?" Myers became angry again, about to slap Sha'nae.

Darius suddenly appeared around the corner. "Don't hit her, man. You know Elder doesn't want anything to happen to her. She was the first success. Now, there's a chance to do more. Sha'nae can't be damaged."

Myers shook her head. "Stankin heifa hit me upside the head with a bedpan. Why can't I get my lick back? My head still hurts." Myers was complaining again. Now, her voice was becoming kind of high-pitched. It was giving Sha'nae a massive migraine.

Sha'nae was frustrated.

"Put...the...shut...to...the...up!!!"

Myers raised her hand to hit Sha'nae. Darius pushed her out of the way. He pushed Sha'nae the rest of the way to wherever they were going. Sha'nae was so out of it that she ignored how they got to the building and didn't know what floor they were on. She wanted to text Sha'ree and tell her what was going on, but she couldn't put her and the babies in harm's way. Sha'nae trusted her twin had had enough time to get as far away as possible.

"Where are the babies, Sha'nae? We need those kids." Darius started to question Sha'nae as they moved along.

Sha'nae shook her head. She honestly didn't know where Sha'ree had taken the twins. That was the point of sending her ahead and choosing to stay behind. There would be little to no danger. The less Sha'nae knew, the better.

Darius was starting to become angry with her. He knew that she had to know something about where the twins were. Elder wanted those babies. He had paid a nice amount of money to use Sha'nae's uterus to carry the future. Elder never explained the future, but for 1.2 billion dollars, Darius would have sold his mother. And he got to have Nurse Myers.

They had finally arrived at the office. The secretary gave Sha'nae the side eye. Sha'nae didn't like her already. The secretary oddly looked a lot like Myers. Sha'nae made a realization. The secretary and Myers were identical twins. She was getting nervous. There were too many layers to this situation. Sha'nae started to become scared. She was drugged and in the hands of her husband

and his girlfriend, who hated Sha'nae's very existence.

Darius walked past the secretary without paying her any attention. He wheeled Sha'nae to a heavy-looking wooden door at the back of the office. There was no noise coming from the room. Myers looked at the secretary, then nodded over at Sha'nae.

"Is Elder in? This heifa is getting on my nerves. I'm ready for her to be destroyed!!" Myers was fuming at this point. "Hurry up and let him know we're here."

Sha'nae realized that Myers was jealous. But why? She already had Darius. Sha'nae realized she was in danger and no one could save her.

Suddenly, the heavy door opened. Sha'nae's heart dropped. She looked up to see a man who was about 6'5" tall. His skin was almost red in color. His face wasn't hard, but it didn't look like he smiled often. The expression on his face was one of irritation and dismissal. Sha'nae felt the man looked like someone she knew, but she couldn't place where. Yet, looking into his eyes, she had a deadly revelation. His eyes were the exact same color as her sons.

"Hello, Sha'nae. It's about time you came back. Why would you not bring the babies with you?

Aren't they why you're here?" The man looked down at her. His voice sounded caring, but his body language said anything but. "Oh, you can't answer me, can you? Sorry about drugging you. I needed to make sure you couldn't run away, though. You're very disobedient."

Darius was watching Elder's face. He found it odd that he was so into Sha'nae. She wasn't anything special. It didn't take Darius long to make Sha'nae fall in love with him. In all honesty, he would have rather had her twin. Sha'ree was the firecracker whose slick mouth could make any man bow to her. Sha'nae was more docile. She would do anything she was asked. That's how Darius was able to get her to go for fertility treatments. He told Sha'nae that he wasn't able to have children. Elder had someone approach Darius about Sha'nae long before he met her. He heard millions of dollars and wasn't listening to anything else. Darius thought he could win over Sha'ree and use her instead, but she was dating his adopted brother Xavior, and he wouldn't let Darius get anywhere near Sha'ree. That was one less headache for Darius now. He was the one who made Xavior's helicopter explode. Granted, Elder didn't know about this. Xavior wasn't loved as much by Elder. He treated Xavior as if he didn't deserve to exist. Xavier's twin, Xavion, got on Darius' nerves too. He never stopped reminding Darius that he was an orphan and that Elder only took him in because he and Xavior wanted a sibling. When Darius was done, Xavion would end up the same way his identical twin did.

"Darius, what's on your mind, son?" Elder glanced over at him.

"Nothing Elder. I'm just ready to get this over with. She's not going to tell us where the babies are. What do you want us to do next?" Darius was ready to leave the office. It felt like the temperature in the room had dropped, and Darius didn't know why. He glanced over at Myers, who was shivering also. Darius looked back over at Elder.

"Why are you shivering, Myers? Are you a little cold? You too, Darius? Here, let me help you warm up." Elder walked toward his desk.

Sha'nae's eyes widened in horror as she heard two thumps behind her. She still couldn't move because of the drugs in her system. Sha'nae wanted more than anything to run out of the room, the city, the state. She tried to take her babies and disappear. Tears began running down her face as she screamed inside her head in fear.

"It's ok, darling. I promise everything is going to be ok." Elder walked past the parked wheelchair and closed the office door. "Now, let's see if we can locate those babies."

Oil

Sha'ree pulled into the gas station in a small city named Videl. She hadn't taken any time to stop yet out of fear she could be traced. Blessedly, the twins had slept the entire time. When Sha'ree sniffed the air, she almost threw up. One of the twins had let go, and it was rank. She looked in the back. "Which one of y'all did that? You know you nasty, right? Just passing gas and taking dumps in my car. This ain't no bathroom."

Both of the twins looked at Sha'ree with their purple eyes wide. She felt so frustrated and scared. Sha'ree lost contact with Sha'nae once she had left the Covenant city limits. There were a lot of trees and country. Sha'ree considered contacting her parents but didn't want to bring them added threats. Sha'nae's sacrifice was dangerous enough. Their parents didn't know about the marriage, pregnancy, or birth of the twins. Sha'ree needed to keep things low until she knew what was happening with her sister. Richard and Tonya intensely disliked Darius. Based on what Sha'ree had seen at the hospital, her parents had every right to feel like they did.

Sha'ree walked to the back of the SUV, opening the door behind the driver's side where

Maison was. She opened the door, cooing to him. He looked at her face, then scrunched up his. Sha'ree realized that even though she looked just like her sister, she did not have the same scent, and Maison knew it. Sha'ree dug into the baby bag and found a sweater from Sha'nae. She put it on, then took Maison out of his seat. He inhaled deeply, his tears calming. Chaison looked at them both, waiting for his turn to be picked up. Sha'ree found it odd that even though the boys were only a few days old, they were very emotional and attentive. She knew babies could be advanced, but not that advanced. Sha'ree knew she would need to take the babies for a checkup as soon as possible. She would have to be careful. The twins may end up being reported missing by their biological father. No one knew that Sha'ree had the twins at that point, and the fewer people who knew, the better.

  The babies were finally cleaned and changed. Sha'ree put them in the dual front and back carriers, then headed inside the store to make and warm up the bottles. She would have to withdraw some cash, so there would be less digital trail. She also needed to figure out exactly where they were going. When Xavior was alive, he placed several houses in Sha'ree's name so that if they ever needed a safe home, they would never have to go to the same one twice for an extended period. It also allowed Xavior to hide the properties from his father and brother. Sha'ree never understood why Xavior was so suspicious of them until she received the phone call that Xavior's helicopter had gone down, and there were no survivors. That day, everything inside her broke. That's also the day she went into premature labor with their son. She and Xavior married for a year, and Sha'ree had been 7 months pregnant with their first baby. The day Xavior died, Sha'ree felt she had been stabbed in the heart twice. She delivered their son after going into preterm labor, and she never even got to hold.

    Sha'ree came back to reality. She could do nothing about the past. Right now, her twin trusted her to care for her nephews and keep them safe. She would do for them what she couldn't do for her son and Xavior. Sha'ree was going to make sure her nephews were safe and stayed safe. She wiped the tears from her face, wiping away the pain of the past year. When she glanced down at Maison in the front carrier, his face was solemn and intent, as if he was trying to figure her out. "Hey, little one." Sha'ree cooed to Maison. "Please don't show out when we go in this store. I don't know what it is with you, but you are definitely the most defiant one of the two of you. Why can't you be chill like Chaison? You see how quiet he is? He doesn't do all the fussin' and huffin'. Get like your brother."

Maison continued to stare into Sha'ree's eyes. Chaison chose that moment to sneeze on the back of her neck. Sha'ree was shocked and amused at the same time. These babies were something else. Sha'ree walked into the store, shaking her head. The person behind the counter looked at Sha'ree strangely but said nothing. Sha'ree first went to the drink cooler since the boys weren't fussing. She figured they could wait a few more minutes. She turned to the snack aisle right behind her. Sha'ree glanced into the mirror in the corner above her. She noticed the cashier watching her and on the phone. She realized she needed to hurry up and leave. She was starting to feel nervous. Sha'ree popped the boys' bottles in the microwave, hoping they would warm quickly. She didn't need either to end up with colic because the milk was cold. Once the microwave dinged, Sha'ree hurried to the counter with her items. "Hey, baby doll. What's your rush?" The cashier asked.

"I have two babies strapped to me. What do you think my rush is?" Sha'ree retorted. She was starting to feel annoyed. The man was asking too many questions already, even though it had been only one question. Sha'ree felt the need to get back on the road quickly. "I'm kind of in a hurry. Can you please hurry up just a little? I know my babies are ready to eat, too."

The cashier grunted and moved a little faster. Sha'ree kept glancing outside, hoping no other vehicles would pull up. She didn't even listen for the total; she just handed the cashier a $20 bill and waited for her change. Sha'ree felt trapped in the store and needed to get out. Her heart was racing, and the babies were anxious because her attitude had changed. The cashier kept glancing outside, too.

"Here's your change. Have a great day." The cashier tried to be polite, but Sha'ree could hear the attitude in his voice.

"Thank you. Have a great day." Sha'ree hurried back out to the SUV. She glanced back to see if the cashier was watching, which he was from the doorway. Fortunately, Sha'ree had enough sense that when she pulled into the gas station, the SUV was turned the other way so the license plate couldn't be seen. She knew she had enough gas to reach a few more cities. Sha'ree did not want to stay at that station any longer. She placed both boys back in their car seats, then propped up their bottles. She hurried and drove off, glancing in the rearview mirror to ensure no one was coming behind her. Sha'ree couldn't relax until she reached the highway. There were still a lot of back roads to travel. She tried to speed without drawing attention to herself. Sha'ree slowed down some as a police car pulled up behind her. She was hoping that they didn't cut their lights on. The officer sped up behind her, then passed her, looking at her annoyingly. Sha'ree would instead take that chance. Eventually, she reached the highway. After a few miles, Sha'ree stopped at a gas station to get gas, change the babies, and burp them.

  Sha'ree pulled into Chiva about three hours later. She was exhausted, and Chaison and Maison were starting to get fussy. They pulled off onto a dirt road. The house they were pulling up to was surrounded by a security gate that couldn't be seen from the main road. The house was brick and beige. This was one of the houses Xavior had placed in Sha'ree's name. She was going to sell it at one point but felt the urge to keep it just in case. She was glad she didn't. Sha'ree ensured the gate had locked, then used her phone to lock in the code to unlock the house's front door. Xavior had made sure that the house came with all the security needed. With him fighting against his father and not trusting his twin, he wanted to be sure that Sha'ree and their son were safe.

"Come on, little ones. It's time to go in the house and get some rest. I don't know what's going on with your mom. My chest is aching like something has happened to her." Sha'ree was talking to the boys, who weren't even paying her attention. Maison looked like he was about to pitch his 5th fit of the day. Chaison was trying to figure out where they were and trying to see everything around him. Sha'ree placed the car seats on the floor in the living room, then went back to the SUV to get the rest of the stuff out. She realized she would have to get some baby pods to wash the baby's clothes. She mentally noted the extra things she would need since Sha'nae only told her a few things to grab. Sha'ree still had the crib from her son, so she placed the babies in it, turned on the monitor, and prepared to nap before the next time the boys needed to eat.

Trim the Ends

While Sha'ree was taking the babies in, she didn't notice there was someone not far from the property. Xavior had driven discreetly from the hospital after Sha'nae was taken. He had to make sure the babies were ok. His heart was hurting so bad, staring at Sha'ree and the babies. Xavier knew that she was still hurting inside from losing their son. He wished he could have been there for her. Yet no one could know he was still alive. Xavior wouldn't have shown himself to Sha'nae, but their handler required him to contact her. He was the only one who knew she was undercover.

Xavior stayed a little longer, then walked back through the woods to his car. He glanced both ways before heading down the dark dirt road, then turned towards the highway. The GPS kicked on, and Xavior entered the coordinates to the house where he was to attend a meeting about the next target. There were so many things he had not and could not tell Sha'ree about his life. It was a secret that could only be said at the right time, and that time wasn't coming up anytime soon. Xavior also had to keep an eye out for Xavion. The problem with having an identical twin is you could feel each other. Xavior knew when Xavion was on the move, and he could tell when he was getting frustrated or upset. He knew something that his twin didn't, though.

When Xavior and Xavion were born, Elder had a chip placed in both of them. It allowed him to track them at all times. When Elder found and adopted Darius, a chip was placed in him, too. Elder wanted all three of them to find the Virus and the Cure. The combination and procreation of this man and woman would create a race of people who could never die. Or so it was believed. The theory still hadn't been tested yet, and the Company that Xavior had become an agent of was trying to eliminate any possibility of it being tested. The Company knew the Covenant was attempting to engineer the Virus and the Cure. Hence, the purpose of the artificial semination of various women, with Elder being the head and only male donor. He believed that his DNA was enough to create the perfect humans. This wasn't to save mankind, though. Elder believed he was a god and that all mankind should come from him.

When the Company approached Xavior, he was already looking for a way to stop his father from bioengineering the Virus and the Cure. He gladly joined them but didn't let his father and brother know he had defected from the Covenant. He needed to remain privy to everything and information that could be gained. The thing was, it seemed Darius had a huge trust issue. Plus, he had a huge crush on Sha'ree. He tried to vie for her attention from Xavior, but in Sha'ree's eyes, Darius never existed, which made him very angry. Darius didn't know that his people didn't appreciate how he treated them, so it wasn't hard for Xavior to find someone to give him inside information about Darius. He learned of Darius' plot to kill him yet still let it happen. Darius wasn't as brilliant as he thought he was. Xavior let it slide, though. When he got his payback, Darius, Elder, and Xavion were all going to pay for what they did to him, Sha'ree, and their son.

    Xavior pulled up to the library and parked near the back entrance. He saw only three other cars there, so the meeting would be short and to the point. As he walked into the building, Xavior began to wonder why the Company picked him, and at the time they did. Something seemed so familiar about the leader of the Company. She was an older woman, around her late 40s or early 50s. She was very motherly, especially towards Xavior. Everyone called her Ms M or Lady M. Xavior could never figure her out. No one knew where she came from or her real name. There were plenty of rumors to go around, though. Everyone thought she may have entered the Company as a spy or undercover agent who worked her way to the top. There were also rumors that she had married before and that her husband had abandoned her. Lady M would never talk about herself. If anyone would try to ask questions or dig deeper into her life, Lady M would immediately change the subject or walk away. Xavior wondered if he could get M to open up to him one day.

    Xavior walked into the library, nodding to the librarian behind the counter. She leaned her head toward the back conference room. The lights inside were dim. Xavior walked in and allowed his eyes to adjust. He knew where everyone was in the room. Lady M would be more towards the front of the room near the projector. Justin would be closer to the door. The man always seemed like he was in a hurry and ready to run at any point in time. Sha'nae would typically be by Lady M, but as she was undercover in the Covenant, Monica, Lady M's assistant, was in her place. Another agent Xavior had never met was there. He looked at Lady M for an explanation.

"X, this is Adrian. He's a scientist at the Covenant lab. He was involved in the IVF transplant for Sha'nae. Unfortunately, he was being watched by Elder's men, so there was no way for Adrian to warn us of what Elder would do to her." Lady M slammed her fist on the table. The agents had seen her get angry, but never that angry. She loved Sha'nae like a daughter, which was why Xavior and Sha'ree found each other. Lady M treated every agent like a family member, and that's why the Company had grown so quickly. It wasn't just an undercover agency but an agency that helped women and men escape safely from abusive relationships. There were libraries, stores, salons, and other businesses and government branches that provided safety, housing, cars, money, and travel. Lady M had taken the Company and made it more than any predecessor had conceived or imagined. Adam cleared his throat. "I'm sorry that I couldn't do more for Sha'nae."

"It's not your fault. I couldn't do much for her either," Xavier shook his head. He couldn't be there for Sha'ree, but he at least wanted her to have her twin close by her side through everything. Sha'nae could keep Sha'ree together until Xavior could safely show himself to her again. It was why Lady M had picked him as a handler for

Sha'ree. What wasn't expected was Darius. That dude was always in the way, and Xavior was sick of him. He couldn't touch him without alerting Elder to what was going on. He believed his twin was in on some things regarding Darius, too. But Xavior didn't have the evidence needed.

"Ahem!! Agent X, where is your mind at?' Lady M cleared her throat. She knew that X was struggling to focus, not with just everything that was going on, but healing from the loss of his son. Lady M wished she could tell X certain things, but if she did, it would blow the whole mission. She needed him focused and on his job. Maybe later, the whole truth could be revealed. Right now, they needed to figure out how to get Sha'nae out of Elder's hands and back to her babies. At the same time, they had to ensure the twins' safety. If Elder got his hands on them, he would change the trajectory of human history. Elder created twins with DNA that was necessary to alter humans genetically. They were the first humans born who could never get sick, and it was almost impossible for them to die. Lady M and the Company were bent upon never allowing Elder and the Covenant to get the kind of access nor use their lab to create more people like the twins. No one understood this mission and how it would change the entire world's lives if Elder weren't stopped.

***

Sha'nae awoke in a bed not her own. The last thing she remembered was the sound of Darius and Myer's bodies hitting the floor. She didn't know Elder did, but she believed both of them were dead. Sha'nae couldn't shake the eerie feeling that she would suffer the same fate if she didn't tell Elder where the babies were. She didn't care, though. She was fine as long as her sons were safe and hidden from Elder and anyone else who wanted to use them.
"I see we're awake now." A voice said next to Sha'ree. Sha'ree shuddered, knowing exactly who that voice belonged to. "Long time no see, little sister." Xavion's voice spoke softly, but there was also steel in it.

Sha'ree nor Sha'nae liked Xavion. Something about him always seemed off. Plus, he was always in competition with Xavior. Anything Xavior did, Xavion wanted to prove he could do it better. It didn't help that Elder favored Xavion over Xavior. In his eyes, he did no wrong.
Sha'nae was trying to figure out why Xavion was

even sitting there, as he always gave his attention to and chased after Sha'nae.

"Do you know where you are?" Xavion questioned.

"No. Where am I?" Sha'nae bit back with an attitude. She was so tired of the questions and being trapped in this building.

"You're in the lab. Elder wants to see what kind of condition you're in so he can do another implantation on you." Xavion had a cocky smile on his face that didn't reach his eyes. Like his father, his eyes were cold. Sha'nae kept the shiver that ran up her spine from showing on her face. Being near Xavion made her want to vomit. Xavion reached out to touch her face. Sha'nae flinched unconsciously

"Am I that bad?" Xavion questioned. "All I want to do is be here for you. I want Sha'ree. Why couldn't she let me in? Why did you have to pick Xavior?"

"Because he pursued her. But your brother is dead. So why are you still angry?" Sha'nae retorted, anger dripping from her voice.

"And? He's my twin. He still didn't deserve Sha'ree. He took her from me." Xavion was starting to get angry.

Sha'nae snorted. "Since when did she belong to you for him to steal her from you? I think you may be as crazy as your father. I heard he did something to your mom; that's why she isn't here anymore." Sha'nae knew she was pushing buttons, but she didn't care. It didn't look like she was going anywhere anytime soon, so she might as well have fun while she was at it.

Xavion's face became dark and twisted. "I always knew you were just as spicy as your twin. Do you know why my father chose you to have my little brothers?"

Sha'nae realized the strangeness of the situation as Xavion made his statement. Her sons were his and Xavior's brothers. Which also made them Darius' adopted brothers. What kind of twisted…then another realization hit Sha'nae. She looked into Xavion's eyes, noticing the one gold and one purple eye. Her stomach began to churn, and she leaned over to vomit off the side of the bed.

Xavion began to chuckle. "Well, Elder, I think she's starting to figure things out."

"I noticed. I saw the wheels in her mind start to turn as you began explaining things." Elder stepped into the room, seemingly cold air following him. "Congratulations Sha'nae. You're going to be the grandmother of the perfect species of humans." Sha'nae vomited again, realizing that she was indeed chosen for a reason.

"Why me?" Sha'nae asked, wiping her mouth with the corner of the blanket, then scooting across the bed to get away from Elder and Xavion.

"You have the perfect DNA: you and your twin. You were both born with a gene named GSN-20, which allows for rapid healing. Why do you think when you all hurt yourselves, it would heal in a matter of minutes, with no scars? Your parents knew about this because you were engineered in the same lab your twins were." Elder explained, watching for Sha'nae's reaction.

    She couldn't believe it. There was no way that she and her sister were just randomly created. There had to be more to this than that. Sha'nae wrecked her brain to ask the right questions, but at the same time, her mind was muddled by the heaviness of the information just poured on her. What had she and Sha'ree's parents been hiding? Why had they never told them? How were their parents even part of the Covenant? As Sha'nae tried to gather her thoughts, her parents walked in. She looked at them and began having a panic attack. As the room became dark around her, Sha'nae heard her father say, "It's time, daughter."

Discuss a Style

  Several years had passed. Chaison and Maison were now five years old. Sha'ree hadn't heard from her sister or parents. It was like everyone had disappeared. She took on the role of mother to her nephews with no problem. Chaison was a bright, well-behaved, yet somewhat shy child. Maison, on the other hand, seemed always to be angry about something. He wanted complete control of everything. Chaison could do nothing without Maison bossing him around. Chaison followed his twin like a puppy, though. If Maison wanted to have or do something, Chaison had his back as a brother and twin should.

  Sha'ree didn't like this attitude, though. She knew Maison was using his brother on purpose. Sha'nae had tried to break Maison acting that way toward his twin, but nothing worked. Daycare was a nightmare also. Maison refused to get along with the other kids in their class. Chaison got along with almost everyone. But if Maison said he didn't like someone, he expected Chaison to act the same, no matter how Chaison felt. Sha'ree felt so frustrated. She was getting calls almost daily about how Maison was acting.

As the twins grew older, Sha'ree realized that she may not be able to keep them hidden as much anymore. Everyone around Chiva was discussing their strangely colored eyes. They also talked about how mean Maison was compared to how sweet Chaison was. Sha'ree was scared that she wouldn't be able to protect them anymore. She wanted to send them away, but with no contact with her parents and the lost communication with Sha'nae, Sha'ree had nowhere to send Maison and Chaison. She made up her mind that once they were old enough to take care of themselves, she was going to leave. It was a tough decision, but it was the only other way Sha'ree could think of that would give the Covenant another trail to sniff and keep them away from her nephews. With all her heart, she wished that Xavior was still around to help her through this.

    The school year went on, with a new event almost every day. One day, Maison broke his hand, punching a wall because he was angry at another student. Sha'ree rushed to the hospital to check on him.

"Why would you do that? What were you thinking?" Sha'ree asked.

Maison stared into her eyes. "It was with the wall or him. I'm tired of Wallace thinking he can pick on Chaison every day. I'm the only one who can beat up and pick on my brother. They better be glad it was a wall and not Wallace's face."

Sha'ree shook her head, then turned to Chaison. She noticed he grimaced in pain, even though he hadn't hit anything. Sha'nae realized Chaison and Maison's connection was more profound than hers and Sha'nae's. Chaison felt everything Maison did. She wondered if Maison could feel Chaison's pain. It seemed like the boy never felt pain since he was always doing something painful or violent yet never cried or showed evidence of pain. Sha'ree was starting to wonder what kind of child her sister birthed. She thought about taking the twins to therapy to see if they needed something, especially Maison. Sha'ree was afraid for everyone's life around him. He had yet to hurt anyone physically, but you could never be too careful, especially with Elder as their father and Xavion as their brother.

It felt weird to think that Xavior and Xavion were Maison and Chaison's brothers. Sha'ree didn't understand what was going on. She didn't know how to get to the bottom of what was happening. If Sha'ree started digging too much, it could expose her and the twins. There had to be a way to find out what was happening without alerting the Covenant or Elder. Maison was going to make it challenging to get the information, also. There was no one to contact to help except Donald.

      Donald Michaelson was a friend Sha'ree had made while in Chiva. Sha'ree knew Donald had a crush on her. She felt like it was time to move on from Xavior. Sha'ree had held on to the pain for too long. She knew she would probably never have another child after losing her and Xavior's son. She knew that she needed help and would eventually leave Maison and Chaison. Sha'ree was planning how she would explain things to Sha'ree if that time ever came. Her heart hurt being without her twin. One thing her heart and mind did know was that Sha'ree was still alive. What condition she was in was a different question. But that may never be determined. Sha'ree just needed to keep moving until things were solved.

***

      Donald sat across from Lady M at the table in the local Chiva diner. He was about 28 years old, with light brown hair and eyes. His skin was bronze-toned. Donald was a Yale graduate and a bioengineer. The Company had recruited him to help keep an eye on Sha'nae and infiltrate the Covenant as a scientist along with his best friend, Justin. Justin had just gotten married and had a little girl on the way. They had worked for the Company for almost 6 years and had been at the Covenant fertility treatment center for nearly 2 years. The lab had complete and total trust in them, so Donald and Justin had more freedom than other scientists. Their experience and expertise in bioengineering made them necessary and the joint head of the lab and research section.

      Justin was sitting next to Donald, his nerves on edge. He couldn't believe what Lady M was asking. He and Donald knew that Xavior was still alive. Lady M was asking Donald not only to recruit Sha'ree but also to marry her. Donald was afraid, fear written all over his face. He knew they would not live long if Xavior ever found out what Lady M had put him and Justin up to.

"I know what you're asking. Why me, though?" Donald had fear laced in his voice.

Lady M looked Donald straight in the eye. "Because you're the best cover. You have already worked with the Covenant in the lab with Justin and Adrian. Sha'ree will trust you. You're already in good with her. And it makes it easier to keep an eye on the twins and her."

Donald knew the main reason Lady M wanted him near Sha'ree e was for the twins. But he liked her as a person. She was beautiful, intelligent, and dedicated to her sister and nephews. Donald knew she would make a great mother. He also knew that recruiting her would be a daunting task. Sha'ree wasn't the easiest person to get along with when she sank her teeth into something. Donald had watched her around Chiva when she had to go to the school for Chaison and Maison. He'd also watched when she ate Maison up for showing out in school. Donald feared her just a bit. Ok…he feared Sha'ree a lot. But she was worth the fear. Sha'ree was worth anything to Donald. He would do anything for her, even if that meant facing Xavior if he ever found out. Lady M seemed to know what Donald was thinking because she called him out.

"Donald, we cannot afford you to become too entangled with Sha'ree. This is about protecting her and the twins. Not for you to fall in love with her and keep her. Xavier will hurt you about her; you know he won't think twice about it. Honestly, I'll hurt you too. Don't let this mission take you too far." Lady M's face said she was not playing any games.

Donald and Justin looked at each other. Justin knows how Donald feels about Sha'ree. He also knew that Xavion was a huge problem. He and Donald needed to be close to the situation without technically interfering. Yet, interfering was the only way to complete the mission. Donald needed to get close to Sha'ree without Lady M finding out how far he would go. He also needed a good cover in case Xavior caught him.

"I understand," Donald agreed. "I will do my best to protect the twins and Sha'ree. I will also try to persuade her to join us."

"Good. Then I'm leaving this in your hands. You and Justin ensure your stories are straight so Sha'ree can't catch you in any lies. She's a better detector than a lie detector. And you know Sha'ree is the best." Lady M didn't want to trust Donald and Justin with this mission, but she had no choice. Xavior couldn't be seen, and there was no way to make Sha'ree stay away from him if she found out he was still alive. Lady M hated going behind agent's backs, but there was no choice in this situation. Too many lives needed to be protected. She got up from the table, careful with her moves. Once Lady M had gotten into her vehicle, she made the call.

"I need Xavior transferred for a while. Put him on something else. I just gave Donald an assignment, and if Xavior finds out, he will ruin the mission." Lady M's voice was stark and straightforward. The voice on the other end answered,
"Understood, Lady M. Do you want his transfer local or overseas?"
"Send him overseas," Lady M instructed. "Make sure it's a long-term mission, nothing less than 5 years. Execute the orders within the next 24 hours. I want him on a plane in the next 36 to 48 hours."
"Yes, ma'am. Are there any other instructions?" The voice asked the sound of typing in the background.
Lady M closed her eyes and then answered. "I need you to patch through some information for Donald Michaelson. Also, include everything on Sha'ree Duchess. She will be our next recruit and must go undercover once she agrees to come aboard. I also need someone to watch her nephews, Chaison and Maison. At some point shortly, Sha'ree will have to leave them, and they will need guidance. This is all." Lady M disconnected the call, her head starting to pound. So many things were happening, and the stress was getting to her. As Donald, Justin, and Adrian worked in the Covenant lab, they also created a

counteractive product to stop Elder's mission. The issue was that the Elder allowed them only so much information. That man trusted no one. And no one included his children. No progress was being made to find the final plan and stop it.

    Lady M was also glad not to have to face Elder. If he knew what she did, she didn't know if she would still be alive right now. Especially considering he had already tried to get rid of her once. Lady M wanted revenge, but first, she had to save the world. She kept a low profile intentionally. If word got out who she was and what part she played in the bioengineering of perfect or almost perfect humans, Lady M would be tossed in a lab or removed from the face of the earth. Either way, Elder could not remain in control. Lady M did feel like Elder was not alone in this. Someone else was on the field, but no one could see who. Someone needed to go deeper undercover in the Covenant. The question was who to send. Most of the people under her command were either already infiltrating the Covenant or couldn't be placed near anything dealing with the Covenant for the sake of their lives. She was going to figure it out, though. As Lady M pulled off, she glanced in her rearview mirror. Behind her was a burgundy car. She knew that car anywhere. Xion was following her.

***

Sha'ree had spent yet another day at Chaison and Maison's school. Maison could not seem to get things together. He had again hurt himself trying to defend Chaison. Chaison said that Maison was hurt because he got angry over the teacher telling him to stop acting up in class, and he didn't like it. Sha'ree felt like she was at the end of her rope. Her parents and sister still could not be found. There was so much on her shoulders, and she didn't know how much more she could handle. Donald was a big help, though.

Donald had been coming around for about a couple of months. He showed great interest in Sha'ree, Chaison, and Maison. He didn't overdo it. Donald would take the boys to baseball and basketball games. He was very protective of them. Sha'ree didn't know why, but it felt like Donald was intentionally in their lives. He would only be there for her if he had a choice. However, Sha'ree didn't want to argue because help was needed. Donald would also get on Maison for acting up in school. He got Chaison and Maison on the local little league baseball team to interact more with other children to help Maison better control his attitude. Granted, it only worked to a certain extent. Maison would not let go of his unpleasant attitude any time soon.

  Sha'ree had taken the twins to the park so they could run off some energy before they went home to do homework. She had decided to start working on the boys' birthday party as they ran around. A shadow fell across her on the bench she was sitting on.

"Well, hello, beautiful," Donald's cheerful voice rang.

"Hey, Don. What brings you by?" Sha'ree looked up, having smelled his cologne as he neared her.

"Saw you and the boys here and just wanted to check on y'all," Donald answered. "I also wanted to see if you would go on a date with me. My friend Justin and his wife are willing to babysit. They have a baby and need all the practice they can get."

Sha'ree considered the invitation. She hadn't been on a date since the death of Xavior. "Sure. Why not? I haven't been on a date in a while. It would be good to get away from the boys for a little while."

Sha'ree didn't know that the date was not as much about her as it was about Justin being able to ask the boys some questions. Donald had observed some things about Chaison and Maison. The main thing was that the boys could heal quickly and were extremely intelligent. Chaison had some of the highest scores in Kindergarten. Maison's scores could be just as high, but he was more into making his brother do his bidding and beating up people at school.

Donald and Justin had gotten together and decided that the best way to recruit Sha'ree was to get information and try to coax her to join the Company. The boys needed more protection. The Company needed Sha'ree and her skills. Xavior had put a lot of time into training Sha'ree to protect herself and their future children. Granted, neither of them had expected how things went. Donald knew Chaison and Maison were her kryptonite. Especially since it had been so many years since she had contact with Sha'nae. But Donald wasn't the only one with plans for Sha'ree or the twins.

Braided Up

    Sha'nae walked another lap around her room. Elder was not going to let her go after all this time. She had not found a way out of this fortress yet. Elder had tried to do more IVF with Sha'nae, but she had her little tricks. He seemed to have forgotten that biochemistry was Sha'nae's forte. She had asked for aloe vera to treat the wounds that she was giving herself. The aloe vera would induce a miscarriage. In all his intelligence, Elder didn't even understand what Sha'nae was doing.

    Xavion would often visit her, mainly to goad her or attempt to get some information out of her. He knew Sha'nae knew where her sister was. He was sure of it. How could he get Sha'nae to trust him enough? Xavion would bring her little treats and foods that he knew she and Sha'ree liked. At least he did pay that bit of attention. Xavion figured if he could "rescue" Sha'nae, Sha'ree would be with him like she had been with Xavior. Somehow, Xavion was sure Xavior was still alive. It's like he felt his twin at all times. However, he never brought that to Elder's attention because he had plans.

Sha'nae had just finished her tenth lap when Elder walked in. She noticed that he looked pretty stressed and disappointed.
"What do you want now?" Sha'nae asked, smirking as she got ready to do another lap.
"What have you been doing? The IVF should have worked several times by now, but somehow, you are avoiding pregnancy. Something is going on, and you're going to tell me." Elder demanded.
"Even if I were doing something, I would never tell you. I already had one set of children for you. I refuse to give you any more. You already went against my will and mixed up with Darius."
Sha'nae was so tired. She knew Elder wouldn't let her give up As much as she wished he would.
"The sooner you create more children, the sooner you can get out of here. I promise you this." Elder was trying to cajole her but knew he was fighting a losing battle.
"Look, I don't care what your promises are. I'm not giving you more kids, and I'm not giving you my kids. So deal with it." Sha'nae had had enough of Elder's words and presence.
"Fine. Xavion, she is now your problem. You'll figure out how to get me another set of twins. And why haven't you found out what happened to my other babies? I'm getting tired of this." Elder's

face was angry. The man had aged almost a dozen years since kidnapping Sha'ree. His decisions were irrational and desperate. Everyone was hoping the man would be dead before he achieved his dream. Yet, he woke up every day more determined than the day before. Even though he was only around 55-60, Elder's face was weathered from the stress of not being able to finish his "perfect human" project.

Xavion made himself look pitiful in front of Elder. "I'm sorry, Elder. I will fix this as soon as possible and find your twins." Xavion had his plan that he was implementing, and Elder would eventually hate him for it. He relished in that thought. He still wanted to do what Elder did in creating the perfect humans. Yet, Xavion didn't think Elder should be in charge anymore. No one knew that Xavion had done his twist on things. He had so many secrets that the Covenant would never find out about. Elder's time was limited. He just didn't know how limited.

"Well, get on it. I'm tired of my tests being held up. These boys are needed for the final phase. Their genotype and blood can create the perfect person." Elder had finally explained at least part of his plan.

Xavion and Sha'nae looked at one another. Things were getting out of hand. They were stalling as long as possible. Things would have been that much easier if Elder had just died off. But that man proved daily he wasn't going anywhere. Xavion had another plan involving getting Sha'nae out. Not because of Elder, though. He needed her out so she could keep the twins away long enough. As long as Sha'nae was there, there was no way to deal with Elder on the right level. Xavion didn't want to protect Sha'nae, but she would be helpful in his plans.

"I understand Elder. I will do as you ask. Give me some more time." Xavion tried to placate Elder. He could tell the man was buying none of it, though.

"I'm giving you six more months. You'd better come up with something. If Sha'nae won't do her job, I will go after Sha'ree. And I think that's the last thing either of you want." Elder looked pointedly at Xavion and Sha'nae. He knew Sha'ree was a vice for both of them. Elder also knew Xavion still felt some way that Sha'ree had fallen for Xavior over Xavion and that even after Xavior had passed, Sha'ree wouldn't give Xavion the time of day. Elder wanted to use every painful point to get what he wanted. He knew that pain didn't change the DNA sequence, but it could change how Xavion and Sha'nae's genes were expressed or showed up. The perfect human had to come from the worst of pain. And Elder was going to ensure it did…one way or another.

***

Sha'ree had had yet another long day. Maison had caused enough trouble for the whole second grade. That boy was about to get kicked out of school. Chaison was the only reason why Maison was still allowed to come. Now, that child had the smoothest tongue despite being shy. Sha'ree found that Chaison had become well-known for being kind and sweet—the polar opposite of his twin. No one could figure out how they came from the same womb. Granted, Sha' knew the answer, making her skin crawl and craw itch.

Donald had become an even more tremendous help. However, he pushed for a marriage between him and Sha'ree. She had been stalling for the past few years. But it was getting harder and harder. Sha'ree wanted to find her sister first. The twins needed her more than ever. Donald claimed to know where Sha'nae was, but he also said that more research was needed before it could be confirmed. Sha'ree felt like Donald was just trying to keep her around since she wouldn't commit to marrying him. Some part of her wouldn't trust him, and she knew it wouldn't change until she understood why.

Sha'ree pulled to the school, waiting for the boys to get in from the pickup line. She ensured she had snacks and juice because Maison's only thoughts were food when he got in the car. He didn't say hi or anything—no hug for his mom. Just give him the food. Chaison was the one who said hi, checked on Sha'ree's day, and gave her hugs and a kiss before asking for his snack and drink. He was the reason Sha'ree kept fighting through. Maison made her want to dump him on the Covenant's doorstep and let them figure it out. But she also refused to separate the twins. It was like they had a codependency, which Sha'ree found very odd. If one was sick, the other was sick the same way. If Maison were hurt, Chaison would feel the same pain in the same place. This is why everyone believes Maison will hurt himself on purpose. He couldn't physically hurt Chaison but knew he felt his pain.

Sha'ree had had the boys in therapy for a while, especially Maison. Two years, and it seemed like nothing had changed with him. He wasn't meaner or angry, but it hadn't improved either. There had become a fear that he was going to harm someone or himself. The school had tried several times to get Sha'ree to send Maison to a military or alternative school. She refused because that meant sending Chaison, which would not happen in this lifetime or the next.

"Hey, babies!!" Sha'ree greeted the boys as they got in the car.

"Hey, Mom!!" Chaison greeted back. Maison just grunted and reached for his snack.

Sha'ree shook her head. "How was your day? What did you learn?" Chaison answered all her questions. Maison just stared out the window. Sha'ree knew something was heavy on his mind because he had never been that quiet. Just as she was getting ready to ask Maison what was wrong, Sha'ree heard Chaison yell. She whipped her head just in time to see a white truck barrel into the side of their SUV.

     Sha'ree woke up to the sound of beeping. Her head was in shambles. She didn't know what happened or why she hurt so badly. Sha'nae turned to see a man sitting in a chair beside her bed, his head on her leg.

"Excuse me," Sha'ree whispered.

The man hurriedly lifted his head. "Do you want some water?"

"Yeah," Sha'ree's throat felt so dry. It hurts to breathe. Her chest felt like someone had slammed something into it. There was a fog that wouldn't clear in her head. "Umm...who are you and what happened? Why am I here?"

The man handed her a glass of water. "First, drink this." Sha'ree took the water and drank it. "You were in a car accident. It was awful. You have some broken bones, and your face was badly cut."

"Who hit me? Was anyone else hurt?" Sha'ree was starting to freak out. She reached to touch the bandages on her face.

"We don't know who hit you. Wait, do you not remember what happened?" The man began to look at her with concern. He then moved her hands away from her face.

"I honestly don't know anything. I honestly don't even know my name. I don't know why I'm here. I don't know how I got into a car accident. There's this fog in my head, and I can't shake it. Things are so muddled." Sha'ree was starting to panic.

The man looked at her and shook his head. "Lacy, everything is going to be ok. The fog is normal from the accident. Give yourself a few days.

Things were touch and go, but the doctors could bring you back. I promise you, honey, I will take care of you. By the way, I'm your fiancé, Donald." Donald knew he was lying, but he was getting what he wanted. He had Justin give Sha'ree a drug that would permanently block her memory. Donald would complete his mission, his way, on his terms, no matter what Lady M said.
"Ummm...ok." Lacy felt confused by the name, but it sounded right to her. It must be who she was. She thought she could trust Donald.
"I'm going to step out the room and talk to the doctor before he comes to check on you." Donald kissed Lacy on the forehead. Lacy nodded in agreement, then laid back down. Donald walked out the door, exhaling heavily. Xavion was standing right outside.
"It's done. She thinks she's engaged to me. Sha'ree no longer exists. Her name is now Lacy Philips. All the paperwork is complete." Donald explained. Xavion still loved Sha'nae, but for his plan to work, she couldn't exist anymore. He handed Donald the money, then walked to the room where Chaison and Maison were lying. They were going to be reunited with their mom. Yet, they didn't know that she was really their mom. Sha'ree would never exist again. The

woman Xavion had loved for years was officially gone. The hole in his heart was now becoming ice. Time to get his plan rolling.

Beard Gang

    Xavion returned to the Covenant, going straight to Sha'nae's room. He needed to get her out before Elder realized what was happening, and Chaison and Maison woke up. Donald had gotten in touch with Xavion through specific channels. He never said that he worked for the Corporation. Xavion never said he was part of the Covenant. Both men had one common goal: getting what they wanted, no matter what they had to do to get it.

    Xavion had arranged for the truck that hit Sha'ree and the twins. When he saw them, he knew precisely why Elder wanted them. They may have been his little brothers, but Xavion felt no connection to Maison. Chaison felt this odd feeling of protection, as if he would never allow anyone or anything to hurt him. Xavion didn't even feel that toward his own identical twin. This is why he agreed to Donald's plan. Otherwise, he would have done things his way. Granted, he had to give Donald his props. He had things planned out to a T.

    Sha'nae looked up from the bed, shocked to see Xavion. She could tell he had something going on and was nervous about what he was about to do.

"Get ready. In about 15 minutes, I'm getting you out of here." Xavion spoke quietly. He knew that Elder had listening devices in the room. Elder trusted no one. Xavion also did it where the camera couldn't see him, and his lips barely moved. He signed "Hurry up" to Sha'nae, then left. Sha'nae grabbed very little, as she had very little in the room. Elder had taken her phone, so there was no communication for her. She did have a few pictures her parents had given her, trying to placate her into telling where her twin and her sons were. Sha'nae hoped never to see those two people again. They may have claimed to be her and Sha'ree's parents, but they certainly didn't act like it.

  Xavion left Sha'nae's room and headed to the security room. He had several people who worked for him in the office, and he ensured they were on duty that day. Xavion walked in and nodded to the security guard at the computer. The guard uploaded some information into the computer and then pressed enter.

"It's done, Sir. You have about 15 minutes before the feed turns back to normal. I've also changed the schedule for some key members, so they won't be in the hall when you arrive at Ms. Sha'nae's room," The guard said.

Xavion headed back to Sha'nae's room, calculating the building's outline. He knew exactly how long it would take to get Sha'nae out of her room, down the hidden stairs, and to the car he had waiting. As Xavion passed people in the hall, he nodded, trying to seem normal.

"Unlock the door with the code." Xavion spoke into the earpiece to the guard. The door clicked open. "Here. Put these on." Xavion handed Sha'nae a wig, some shades, and a new set of clothes.

Sha'nae hurriedly put on everything handed to her. "So, what's the plan? How are we doing this?" "Just follow my lead. I had a guard change what is seen on the monitors for 15 minutes. When we leave this room, we're going straight to a car I have hidden. Act like you belong here, and there won't be any problems." Xavion walked out the door at a quick pace. Sha'nae followed without following too closely. The halls were oddly empty. Xavion and Sha'nae moved quickly. They reached a wall that seemed to be in the way. Xavion waved his hand across what seemed like a hidden panel, and the wall moved to a secret door. He had Sha'nae walk through first, then he walked through. Xavion and Sha'nae walked to the car parked on the side of the road, away from the building. Sha'nae wondered if there were any cameras. Xavion seemed to have read her mind. "There are cameras, but the guard has already covered our trail. Anyone who checks the cameras right now would think everything is normal. I know you're nervous right now, but everything is ok." Xavion reassured Sha'nae. They climbed into the car and drove off. Sha'nae refused to look back. She wouldn't believe she was free until her sons were back in her arms.

    They drove for the next few hours. Xavion kept glancing in the rearview mirror to ensure they weren't being followed. He knew Sha'nae needed to know the plan's next steps, but he wouldn't explain until after they switched vehicles. Xavion had already bought and kept the first car hidden because Elder required all vehicles at the covenant to have a tracking device. Xavion also knew Elder didn't trust him, especially about the Darius debacle and what had happened to Xavior. No one knew that Darius was still alive. Elder thought he had kept that secret.

    Xavion and Sha'nae arrived in Asdele, pulling into a house on a corner.

"We'll nap for an hour, then head to the final place. Go shower and change clothes. Your room is the one at the end of the hall." Xavion explained, then walked into the house. Sha'nae wasn't too far behind. She was curious about where this house came from but was not about to ask any questions. She was hoping Xavion would give her a phone. Sha'nae wanted to get in contact with Xavior and Lady M. She knew it had been years, and they may have thought she had given up or died during the time she was gone. She just needed them to know she was still alive and sticking to the mission.

 Sha'nae showered, then changed into the clothes Xavion had laid out for her. She didn't know how he knew her size, but he was on point. She lay on the bed, her mind going a hundred miles an hour. Sha'nae was free, at least for now. Something didn't sit right with her, but she wasn't sure what it was. Sha'nae had kept up with her workout while stuck in that room. She started her routine, listening for anything unusual in the eerily quiet house.

 Xavion was down the hall, also listening for anything unusual. His nerves were on edge, which wasn't usual for him. He had trusted Donald, which is something he rarely did. Xavion put no trust in people since they were the very same people who had taken out his brother and tried to take him out, too. He began his workout. Sleep was not coming any time soon. Eventually, Xavion went and knocked on Sha'ree's door. It was time to leave.

They got on the road but in a blue SUV. Sha'nae looked over at Xavion, the silence bothering her.
"So…can you tell me the plan now that we're far enough away and aren't being followed?" The curiosity was killing Sha'ree.
Xavion sighed. "Are you that ready to get rid of the person who just helped you escape?"
"Sir…we don't like each other. Never have. Never will. I don't know why you're helping me. So, whatever you have planned, let's put it out there so I can help you make it work." Sha'nae her head.
"Fine. I know where your children are. You're about to go to them." Xavion explained. Sha'nae almost screamed. She was finally going to be with her babies. She had missed so much with them. Sha'nae's heart was about to explode.
"How…how did you do it? How is this possible?" Sha'nae didn't think she could speak.

Xavion stared straight ahead. "I had to make the biggest sacrifice. Trust me, you had better not make me regret this." Sha'nae was not going to know about her sister. At least not anytime soon. Xavion needed to grieve his choice, and looking at Sha'nae daily would not allow him to do that. No, she needed to be free and with her kids. Especially since Elder would have to stop his plan for the time being. Xavion loved Sha'ree enough to give her to someone else. Her memory was gone. His memory of her would never end.

"Don't worry about it. Just know that you're free. I've arranged a home out in the country and a vehicle for you and the twins. You're going to homeschool them for a while. Maison has some anger issues and needs to be away from other kids for a while. Chaison is a wonderful kid. They need each other. The twins are beyond co-dependent. If one stops breathing, I believe the other one will, too. They have a greater connection than me and Xavior had." Xavion explained, glancing to see how Sha'nae was processing things. Her face went from the look of concern to panic and fear. Unfortunately, she was getting tossed into a game she had no idea how to play.

"Do they know who I am?" Sha'nae wondered.

"They think you're Sha'ree, the mother who has raised them. No matter what they do that surprises you, do not show it. This has to go smoothly. Here. These are your ID cards and information. As of right now, you are your twin. Do not tell anyone, and I do mean anyone, any different. If you do, Elder will find you." Xavion was adamant about everything going right, and no one, absolutely no one, was going to mess that up.
"Ok," Sha'nae agreed. "So, I'm now Sha'ree. But where is Sha'ree? Where's my sister?"
Xavion refused to look Sha'nae in the eye. He didn't want her to see his pain. "She's gone for now. She may come back one day. Sha'ree had to go away for a while for this plan to work. No more questions. We're almost to the house."

  They pulled onto a dirt road right outside of Chiva. Xavion pulled the SUV into the driveway of the house Sha'ree had lived in with Chaison and Maison. Sha'ree didn't know that, though. Donald had removed Sha'ree's clothes and anything that was a trace of her. Xavion had given him some clothes and other things he had learned Sha'ree had liked. This had to be pulled off perfectly. The fewer the questions, the better.

  Xavion and Sha'ree walked into the house. It was quiet since the boys had not been released from the hospital yet. The goal was to allow Sha'nae to visit Chaison and Maison a few times in the hospital so they could adjust to one another. Xavion didn't know that Donald had arranged for Maison and Chaison to be given small doses of the memory-suppressing drugs. Justin didn't want to do it, but Donald had given him half of what Xavion had paid him. So Justin was down for whatever. Plus, he had to care for his daughter, and Donald was her godfather. Justin wasn't even supposed to have created the drug, as it was scrapped by Lady M and deemed dangerous. Xavion was going to have an easier time than he thought controlling them.

 Later that day, Xavion drove Sha'nae to the hospital to see Maison and Chaison. Sha'ree could barely contain her excitement. It had been 8 years. 8 long, grueling years. She wondered how much they had grown, what they looked like if maybe their eye color had changed. Sha'ree gained her answer when she arrived at their open hospital room door.

 Two sets of very purple eyes turned to the door. Two heads of curly hair and cute faces turned to Sha'nae. She almost broke down. She looked into two faces practically identical to her and her sister. Maison was sitting on Chaison's

bed, looking stern. Chaison was seated behind him, ready to protect his brother but letting Maison be the first line of defense.
Sha'nae sniffled, then spoke, "Hi, babies. How are you guys feeling?"
"Mom, why do you sound like that?" Chaison questioned.
"Because I'm glad you all are ok." Sha'nae hugged Chaison, then reached for Maison. Surprisingly, Maison allowed her to hug him, although he wouldn't hug her back.
"Who is he, and why does he look a little like us?" Maison was very blunt. He looked curiously at Xavion.
"He's your uncle. He's only visiting for a few days, then he's headed back to his house." Sha'nae spoke of the head of the twins. She mouthed "Thank You" to Xavion. He smiled and nodded, standing guard at the door. At that moment, Donald walked past with Lacy. Xavion and Donald locked eyes. He then looked at Lacy. His mind said it was Sha'ree, but his eyes didn't recognize her face. She also had a little girl whose hand she was holding.
"Come on, baby girl. Let's go home." Lacy said, not paying attention to Xavion standing in the doorway. His heart broke all over again. Xavion

was hoping never to see Sha'ree again. But there she was, belonging to Donald. He turned back around to shut the door hurriedly. Sha'nae's head had whipped to the door hearing Lacy's voice. She thought she had listened to her twin.

"Who was that?" Sha'nae asked. "Her voice sounded familiar."

"No one. Just a couple walking by with their child." Xavion lied. He looked back through the small window on the door, watching the woman he loved disappear out the door.

Fresh

Donald guided Lacy out of the hospital. She was holding Michelle's hand. Donald had convinced Lacy that Michelle was their adopted daughter. Oddly, Lacy felt a connection to the girl. Thinking caused too big of a headache, so Lacy just accepted what she was told. They all got in Donald's car and drove off. Donald took them to his house. He had already arranged for Justin and Christine to create a room for Michelle. Everything had to look believable for the plan to work.

Lady M had been trying to contact Donald, but he avoided her like the plague. He would give her vague updates via Justin. Lady M could destroy the plan also if she knew what was happening. Donald was finally getting what he wanted. He knew it was time for Xavior to return from his long assignment overseas. Donald had to ensure he would not come looking for Sha'ree. Sha'nae was free, and Xavion had paid a large sum. Donald was content.

Donald had talked Justin and Christine into letting him use their daughter Michelle. Granted, Donald had intentionally spent a lot of time with her, so she thought of him as another father. She was also only four, so she didn't know any better. Plus, Justin and Christine adopted a daughter of the same age as Michelle. Christine was dealing with different medical issues and couldn't have another child. What they didn't know was that Donald had also arranged that. He was going to sell the entire lie for as long as possible.

Lacy had been convinced that she worked for the Company. She believed she was an agent and that her being with Donald was an undercover mission. Donald had created a marriage certificate, birth certificate, and any other necessary legal document. He also had a birth certificate and other documents created for Michelle. Few people knew what was happening. If they opened their mouths, there would be dire consequences.

Donald was good at putting on a facade. He could fake anything. He was able to get almost anyone to trust him. He knew who would and wouldn't fall for his lies. Yes, he was a manipulative piece of trash. DONALD DID NOT CARE!! It was all worth it as long as he got what he wanted. He had started attending a local church with the guise of becoming a minister. This was going to be his and Lacy's new cover. Donald wanted to become a pastor in the small town.

Running for office wouldn't be a bad idea either. The more control Donald had, the higher he wanted to attain it.

Lacy and Michelle followed Donald into the beautiful house. It was located on a street with several homes separated by several acres. The area was lovely, with pine and oak trees dotting the land. All the houses had long driveways and gorgeous lawns. Some flowers lined the driveways and bushes around the porches and doors. Donald opened the door and walked Lacy around with Michelle in his arms.

"Are you feeling tired, dear?" Donald asked. "It's almost time for you to take your med."

"I'm good. My face is still sore, but I think it will be ok for now." Lacy answered. The house really didn't feel familiar to her.

"Hey, Michelle. Would you like to give Mommy hugs and kisses to help her feel better?" Donald encouraged Michelle. He put her down, and she ran to Lacy, wrapping her arms around her legs. Lacy bent down, and Michelle placed gentle kisses on her face. Donald smiled. This was going to work out perfectly. "Alright, let me grab your meds."

Lacy followed Donald upstairs to what he said was their room. It didn't feel familiar either.

Lacy figured she would just have to readjust to everything. Donald pulled the meds out of the hospital bag, taking out each pill Lacy needed. There was one set of pills that Lacy ignored. They said multivitamin on them. They were far from multivitamins, though.

"This one is a little bit to take," Lacy said, eying the larger green pill.

"Don't worry about it. I'll get you some juice, and you can break it into that so it doesn't taste bitter and is easier to swallow." Donald went back downstairs to pour the juice. While he was doing that, Lacy began walking around, glancing at pictures. There were pictures of her, her and Donald, photos of their wedding, and pictures of Michelle when she was born. It bothered Lacy that she couldn't remember anything in those pictures. She felt like someone had shut off part of her brain. That headache from trying to focus was returning, so Lacy left it alone. Maybe one day, there would be something that would trigger what she needed to remember.

***

A few days later, Sha'nae took Chaison and Maison home. Chaison was excited to get out of the hospital finally. Maison didn't care either way.

There was nobody to bully on the ward because all the other kids were kept away from him. Sha'nae realized that Maison was going to be a handful. She agreed with Xavion that homeschooling would be the best bet for a while. At least until she could figure out what was going on with Maison.
Sha'nae did notice that he and Xavion had formed a small bond. Their mannerisms were a lot alike also. She also noticed that Chaison was a lot like Xavior. Sha'ree wouldn't say anything about that to Xavion, though, considering he believed his twin was dead. The agreement in the Company was that it would stay that way.

    Sha'nae and Xavion hustled the boys into the house and got them settled. Sha'nae then went into the kitchen to fix them something to eat. She noticed how the kitchen was in her and Sha'ree's favorite colors. Something in Sha'nae's heart broke at that moment, and she let the tears run down her face.
Xavion walked into the kitchen. "Missing Sha'ree?"
Sha'nae nodded. "How is it I'm taking over my sister's life? Why am I taking over her life? So much of this isn't making sense. I'm glad to be back with my babies. Don't get me wrong. But this would be easier with Sha'ree here because she

knows them in a way I don't. This isn't fair!!"
She just let the tears and anger flow. Xavion
considered reaching out to her, but his nature
didn't allow for that much empathy. Plus, if he
allowed the connection to become that close, he
would forget that she was Sha'ree's twin. And
that's a line he never wanted to cross.

Xavion cleared his throat. "You'll be alright.
Give it a couple of days, and you will have
everything together. Here. Here's your new cell
phone. There are very few people who have this
number. No one at the Covenant knows about this
phone. You and the twins are safe for now. I
appreciate that for what it is. Feed the kids, and
make sure they take their meds." Along with the
pain meds from the hospital for the injuries, there
were also some green pills included. "Open the
capsules, put them in some juice, and make sure
the boys take them once a week. Make sure they
don't miss a dose." Sha'nae nodded. "I'm
heading out. I'll grab something from McDonald's
on the way back. I can't stay gone for too long. I
told Elder I was on a short mission, so he hasn't
contacted me yet. He hasn't realized you're gone
since my phone has blown up. Be careful out here.
Don't let anyone in." Xavion walked out the door.

Sha'nae gathered her emotions, then fixed lunch for Chaison and Maison. She would have to learn what they would and wouldn't eat. She had to catch up on their entire lives. Thankfully, Xavion had given her her babies back. But she had to do it through the guise of being her twin. Sha'nae hoped they didn't have to do this for a long time.

***

Xavion checked everything on the property before getting into the SUV. This would be his last visit to Chiva for a while. He knew Elder wouldn't let him go far now that Sha'nae was missing from the Covenant. Xavion loved undermining him. That man may be his father, but Xavion felt he was the reason why his twin was gone and their mother had disappeared. Elder had more secrets than he let on. Xavion did, too. One day, it was all going to come to a head. Xavion couldn't wait to see who was going to win the game.

As Xavion pulled off, a man stepped out of the trees unnoticed. "Well, well. You're changing the players in the game. Let's see what your next move is."

The man's phone rang. "Sir, we've got a few updates. Sha'ree and Sha'nae have been switched. Xavion is dealing with a man named Donald Michaelson, who helped him make the switch. Elder is livid because Sha'nae is gone. Lady M is now untraceable, and we have no idea why." The voice on the phone gave a brief update.

"Sit on Xavion. Elder will find it easy if Michaelson follows since he doesn't have his queen on the board. Lady M will show up when it's time. In the next twenty-four hours, report to me about Sha'nae and Sha'ree." The man said through clenched teeth.

"Yes, sir!!" The voice answered, then disconnected the phone. The man smiled—it was time to start playing his game. The pawns were set, now to arrange the king and queen.

Locced and Loaded Ladies:
Daleigh's Journey
Candi Usher

Janice and Michelle
Candi Usher
MARCUS
Faded Men
Faded Men:
Chaison & Maison

October 3, 2025

December 31, 2025

March 31, 2026

93

Made in the USA
Columbia, SC
01 April 2025